Hedge Hog!

*To Darryl, who taught me about sharing, and
to Kelly, who helped this prickly hedgie grow*

Library and Archives Canada Cataloguing in Publication

Anstee, Ashlyn, author, illustrator
Hedgehog / Ashlyn Anstee.

Issued in print and electronic formats.
ISBN 978-1-77049-991-1 (hardcover).—ISBN 978-1-77049-995-9 (EPUB)

I. Title.

PS8601.N554H43 2018   jC813'.6   C2017-903021-3
                                               C2017-903022-1

Published simultaneously in the United States of America by Tundra Books of Northern New York, an
imprint of Penguin Random House Canada Young Readers, a Penguin Random House Company

Library of Congress Control Number: 2017940553

Edited by Samantha Swenson
The artwork in this book was rendered in gouache, crayon and Photoshop.
Handlettered type by Ashlyn Anstee

Printed and bound in China

www.penguinrandomhouse.ca

1   2   3   4   5   22   21   20   19   18

Penguin Random House
tundra | TUNDRA BOOKS

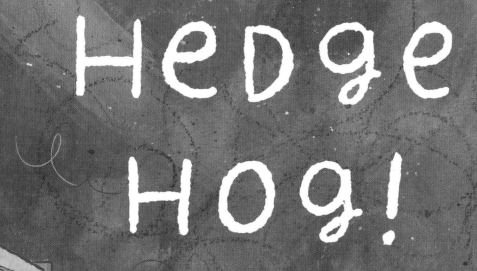

HEDGE
HOG!

ashlyn anstee

tundra

The garden was bustling
with creatures
preparing for the winter.

garden

All the animals were looking
for a place to call home.

The bees and the ladybugs
shared the hive.

The possums moved into
the burrow with the foxes.

The birds and squirrels
found a home in the old oak tree.

And the worms
and the groundhogs
were neighbors!

The hedgehog
lived in the hedge.

All by himself.
He liked it that way.

The grasshopper's home
was under the hedge.

She lived
by herself too.

But then...

DING DONG!

MINE
But soon after...
DING Dong!!
Ding Dong!!!
Ding DONG DING!!
Ding Dong!
DING! DONG!

Under the hedge,
the creatures were settling in.

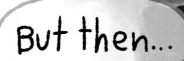

The garden was bustling
as the snow began to fall.